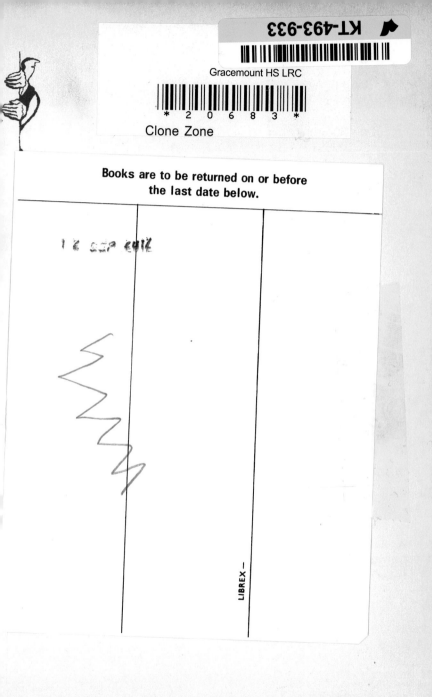

First published in 2001 in Great Britain
by Barrington Stoke Ltd
10 Belford Terrace, Edinburgh EH4 3DQ

Reprinted 2002, 2003

ISBN 1-84299-009-8

Printed by Polestar Wheatons Ltd

A Note from the Author

Like most of my weird ideas, this story started with one too many cups of strong, black coffee. I knew I wanted to write a story about a boy band. What I needed to know was how lifelike did it need to be?

I phoned the publishers.

"It doesn't have to be lifelike at all if you don't want it to be," they said.

"What, so you mean it could be about a band that get abducted by aliens or something?" I said off the top of my head.

There was a pause on the other end of the line. "Yeah, why not?"

And the rest is history.

To me, who would quite like to have been a pop star. Even a rubbish one.

Contents

20683

Chapter 1
Pizza

For Mikey Jones, the floppy-fringed, blond lead singer of rubbish boy band Stud-U-Like, the day began like any other day. He half woke up. He lay in bed. He thought about the World Tour which was coming up soon.
He thought about the endless photo-shoots and the interviews he would have to give.
He thought about his band being number one for the seventh time in a row. He thought about being on *Top Of The Pops* every week and being screamed at by millions of adoring

fans. Then Mikey woke up completely.
"Damn," he muttered.

He tried to tune back into his dream.
He tried every trick in the book. Like closing
his eyes and ... well, that was it really. It didn't
work. Mikey was wide awake. And it had
been such a brilliant dream too.

Mikey decided to treat himself to
breakfast in bed, to try and make himself feel
better. He felt under his pillow. There was
the slice of cold, rubbery pizza he'd left the
night before. It hadn't been cold and rubbery
then, of course. But it was now. When he
was famous he'd lie in his hotel bedroom and
order silver tray-loads of pizza. Every different
sort.

Mikey switched the radio on and took a
bite of the cold pizza. It wasn't easy to chew,
but Mikey comforted himself that this was
the last time. He had made his mind up.
Soon cold pizza would be a thing of the past.

Mikey was like that. Once he'd made up his mind to do something, he did it. Like this whole band thing. When Mikey had seen the advert in the local newsagent's three months ago he had decided there and then that he was going to be a pop star.

The advert had been brief and to the point. 'Wanted for top boy band: Blond One, Funny One, Hard One, Cute One and Other One. Also selection of unused wallpaper and paints for sale. Call 353-7848.'

Mikey had called right away.

"Yeah?" said a gruff voice.

The owner of the voice was 57-year-old Ron Heslop. It was just as well that Mikey couldn't see Ron's dyed, jet black hair, long and curly at the back and short on top. Couldn't see his tinted glasses and cheap gold jewellery. Couldn't smell his revolting aftershave. It was just as well or he might have put the phone down.

"I'm calling about the advert in the newsagent's," said Mikey.

"Wallpaper or paint?" asked Ron.

"Er, boy band actually," said Mikey.

"Oh, right!" said Ron, trying not to sound too astonished. "Which one do you want to be?"

"The Blond One?" said Mikey.

"Are you blond?" asked Ron.

"Not really. But I soon can be," said Mikey.

"Right, well, I'm seeing about 25 Blond Ones so far," Ron lied. "But I'll see if I can fit you in."

"Great!" said Mikey. "When?"

"Today if you like," said Ron.

"Great! What time?" said Mikey.

"What time can you make?" asked Ron.

"Er, now?" said Mikey. "What's the address?"

"Just above the chip shop."

"Which chip shop?"

"The one across from the football ground," Ron told him. "Look, I've got to go. There's someone on the other line." Ron was lying again. There wasn't another line.

Mikey could hardly believe that all that had been nearly three months ago. Three whole months. Boy bands can come and go in that time. There was never any shortage of young, wide-eyed hopefuls, waiting to take their turn and give it their best shot. Mikey Jones was one of them and he didn't care who knew it. He wanted his shot at the big time too. He wanted it bad.

Mikey took another mouthful of rubbery pizza. It would all be different when he was famous though, Mikey was sure of that. All he'd have to do would be to snap his fingers and along would come his personal assistant with a whole selection of pizzas, never cold and never, ever rubbery!

The phone rang. It was Mikey's band mate, Tony.

"All right, Mikey?"

"All right, Tony."

"Sorry, but I can't talk right now."

"Why not?" said Mikey, surprised.

"I said I can't talk right now."

"But *you* phoned *me*. Why did you phone me if you can't talk?"

But it was too late. Tony had already put the phone down. Then Mikey remembered. Tony was The Funny One ...

FACT FILE

Name:	Tony Williams
Age:	18
Height:	5 feet 9 inches in high heels
Hair:	Spiky black with blue streaks
Fave food:	Food!
Fave colour:	Girly colours
Fave joke:	What's brown and sticky? A stick!
Likes:	Girls, chocolate hobnobs and girls
Dislikes:	Sprouts

At first, Mikey had thought he would like to be The Funny One. But then, as he had to admit, he just wasn't funny enough. On a good day he could sometimes raise a laugh – but 'sometimes' wasn't good enough. He'd never been the class clown at school. And he was terrible at remembering jokes.

Mikey had also thought about being The Hard One. But he just wasn't hard enough either. The closest he'd ever got to being in a fight was when the kid from next door snatched his Action Man from him. He stood there for a moment, red and shaking. Then he just ran off and told his Mum. His Mum was no help. She just laughed in his face. Mind you, Mikey *was* nearly sixteen at the time.

No, Scotty was a much better Hard One and Mikey knew it ...

 FACT FILE

Name:	Scotty Campbell
Age:	Who's asking?
Height:	6 feet
Hair:	Shaved
Fave food:	Fish 'n' chips
Fave colour:	Colours are for girls
Fave clothes:	Anything that shows off my 6-pack
Likes:	Working out, going out, being hard
Dislikes:	Stupid questions

Being The Cute One was never an option for Mikey. Oh, he was good looking all right. Those amazing blue eyes. That perfect square jaw. But cute? Nah! You want cute? Lee was cute!

 FACT FILE

Name:	Lee Smith, but you can call me 'L'
Age:	Old enough to be kissed!
Height:	5 feet 3 inches
Ambition:	To be 5 feet 4 inches
Hair:	Mousy brown
Fave food:	Anything my Mum makes
Fave colour:	The colour of my teddy, Mr Bear. He's a kind of faded yellowy-brown. I've had him since I was born.
Likes:	My Mum
Dislikes:	Nothing really, except people who are cruel to little, furry animals

That only left The Other One. The one that nobody ever remembers. No-one wants to be him. Mikey didn't. He'd had quite enough of being forgotten when he was at school. He was always the last one to be picked for football. No, Mikey knew only too well what it was like to be The Other One. And he wasn't ever going to let it happen again.

So it hadn't been hard to choose, really. There *was* no choice. Mikey had to be The Blond One in Stud-U-Like. And quite by chance he'd also become the lead singer. Not that Mikey was great at singing or anything. Far from it. It was just that on a good day he could very nearly sing in tune and not manage to sound like a hippo giving birth. Which is more than can be said for the rest of the band.

Mikey scratched his belly and looked at himself in the mirror. With horror, he noticed a huge pus-filled zit on his perfect, square jaw, like a ... like a ... Mikey couldn't quite think what the zit was like. But then Mikey wasn't one for words. Just as well really, since the band didn't write any of their own songs.

Stud-U-Like were nothing more than a bunch of puppets and Ron pulled all the strings. All they did was look good. Or, in the case of Scotty, look hard. They sang rubbish, old songs first sung by rubbish, old bands way back in the 70s. They didn't know the first thing about music. They were totally talent-free.

Ron Heslop was pretty talent-free himself. So at least the band had one thing in common with their manager. Ron had had a fleeting moment of fame in the early 70s, when he had briefly replaced the bass player in Medicine Lighthouse, best known for their hit, *Groovy Groovy Yeah Yeah!* In fact, *only* known for their hit, *Groovy Groovy Yeah Yeah!*

Mikey squeezed his zit between two fingers. Sploosh! The pus hit the mirror like a ... like a ... well, Mikey couldn't quite think what it hit the mirror like. But it hit it anyway. Mikey looked at his reflection, or rather the bit of his reflection that hadn't been splattered by pus. He saw that his eyes were watering and that a tiny bubble of crimson blood had formed on his perfect square jaw. Mikey couldn't stand the sight of blood. The room started to spin and for a moment he thought he was going to faint.

"Just as well I'm not The Hard One," thought Mikey.

Suddenly a shiver ran through Mikey's body and the dyed blond hairs on the back of his neck stood up. He could hear voices – horrible, tuneless voices, but strangely familiar. Somehow very familiar indeed. What was it? What was going on?

The voices stopped again. Mikey had broken into a cold sweat. His heart was thumping. And then came the words Mikey had dreamed of hearing for so long. The cheesy DJ on the radio saying, "That was Stud-U-Like with their first ever single, *Groovy Groovy Yeah Yeah!*"

Mikey ran to the window and peered through the blinds. Sure enough, there was Kylie, the band's obsessive fan, standing on the other side of the road like she always did, gazing hopefully up at the flat. She was clutching a small radio to her ear, jumping up and down and waving madly at Mikey. Mikey waved back and gave Kylie the thumbs-up. For a moment Kylie looked as if she was about to explode with sheer pleasure.

That's when things started getting really weird. Mikey began to suspect that he was no longer alone in the flat. He began to suspect that someone, or something, was in there with him.

But there was still no clue that very shortly Mikey, along with the rest of Stud-U-Like, would be abducted by aliens. No clue that they would be zapped off to another planet and replaced by a bunch of alien lookalikes.

Mikey turned away from the window, wondering whether to phone his parents, or make himself a cup of coffee.

It would be one of the last things that he remembered.

Chapter 2
Bus

The aliens had been watching Mikey for some time. They'd been watching the rest of the band too. They could watch whoever they wanted to. Whenever they wanted to. They were all-seeing. Nothing went unnoticed.

Everything that Tony, Scotty, Lee or The Other One had been doing had been noted. Their every move had been observed. Their every word had been recorded. Their every thought had been studied. Now the waiting

was over. Now it was time to make a move.
Well, almost time.

The abduction could only happen when all
five members of Stud-U-Like were together at
the same time. One of the main reasons
they'd been chosen in the first place was that
there were five of them. And there were five
aliens. With any luck no-one would even
notice any difference. They all just needed to
be together under the same roof at the same
time, that's all.

But the aliens were not having much luck
getting all five members of Stud-U-Like under
the same roof at the same time. They had
planned to act when the band met up at the
recording studio on Friday morning. But Scotty
was on a Number 12 bus and it got snarled up
in heavy traffic. He was late.

The aliens looked at each other and
started to hum.

be room to swing an alien cat. In the not too distant future, they'd all have to pack their bags and move to another planet. It was the only solution. It was the only way future generations would survive.

The aliens wanted the move to be a peaceful one. They didn't want any hassle. They didn't want to start any intergalactic wars. All they wanted to do was to find another planet they'd like to live on. What was so wrong with that?

The search for a new home had taken a very long time. Just over fifty thousand years in fact. But then it's a pretty big thing if you think about it. Exploring new solar systems and checking out planets takes time. There's a lot of stuff to think about, like is there a decent supply of fresh water? Is there any oxygen? How far is it to the nearest shops?

Anyway, to cut a long story short, in the end, Earth seemed like it could well be the answer. But to make quite sure, the aliens still needed to take a closer look. And they needed to do so without being noticed, which is where Stud-U-Like came in. They just happened to be in the right place at the right time. Or the wrong place at the wrong time. It depended which way you chose to look at it. It depended on whether you considered being zapped through time and space to a distant galaxy a good thing, or a bad thing.

Chapter 3
Pen

When the Number 12 bus finally dropped Scotty off at the studio, things happened fast. Very fast. The actual moment when the band were zapped off to The Planet With No Name took no time at all. It wasn't even a moment. It was less than that. It was instant. The boys didn't feel a thing. They didn't even know anything was happening. One minute they were lazing around, chatting on their mobiles and watching TV, or in the case of Tony, breaking wind and setting fire to it. And the next? They were gone. They were history. Or were they?

Well, yes and no as it happens. It was more a case of now you can see them, now you can *still* see them! Mikey and the rest of Stud-U-Like might have been zapped to the other side of the universe, but a brand new Stud-U-Like had suddenly appeared to take their place. OK, strictly speaking they were just a bunch of clones. But why let a little thing like that get in the way of a boy band getting into the Top 20?

Ron Heslop couldn't tell the difference when he turned up at the studio later on that day. There was 'Mikey', screeching his way through some cheesy, old hit from the early 80s. And there was 'Scotty', 'Tony', 'Lee' and 'The Other One', lying around doing nothing, but looking really good doing it.

In other words, they were doing what they always did. There was no reason at all for Ron to suspect that at that moment the real Stud-U-Like weren't even on the same planet, let alone in the same town.

"You're looking good, lads," said Ron.

The lads, by way of reply, said nothing at all.

"Only a matter of time, only a matter of time," said Ron, rubbing his hands.

The lads said nothing again.

"Before you become famous and I become very rich I mean," Ron went on.

There was a short pause.

"Er, I mean before *we* become very rich of course, lads! *We*!   Not just me!" laughed Ron.

Ron wanted to kick himself. He must watch what he said in the future. They mustn't get the idea that he was ripping them off.

Again, the lads said nothing.

Ron went off, red-faced and in a hurry. Outside the studio, he got into his rusty, old wreck of a car. In Ron's head it really was only a matter of time before Stud-U-Like became famous. It really was only a matter of time before *he* became very rich. It really was only a matter of time before he'd be driving a really flash car. In fact, if Ron had his way, he'd be driving a different coloured flash car for every day of the week!

If only Ron had known he'd just been talking to a bunch of cloned aliens.

Even Kylie, Stud-U-Like's very own obsessive fan, was fooled. She had been waiting outside the studio hoping to see the boys come out.

When they did appear, the guys weren't quite as friendly as usual. They stared right through her. They looked dazed and confused. So what? They had a lot on their minds these days. The stress they were under was enormous. After all, there was every chance that they were about to become superstars. But it was cool. Kylie understood. She knew what the boys were really like. Or at least she thought she did.

So when 'Tony' took her pen and ate it, Kylie didn't bat an eyelid. It was the kind of crazy, wacky thing Tony did all the time. Tony was, after all, The Funny One. He did crazy, wacky things!

Chapter 4
Pants

So that's how the real Stud-U-Like came to be replaced by a bunch of aliens. That's how the bunch of aliens began their stay on Earth, by changing and cloning themselves into a rubbish boy band.

Right now though, the aliens knew nothing about boy bands, rubbish or otherwise. But they soon would. They'd soon find out about all kinds of things. It was their mission

to discover. It was their mission to observe.
It was what they had been sent here to do.

One of the first things the aliens observed
was Kylie. Of course, they didn't know that
she was called Kylie, or that she was
Stud-U-Like's obsessive fan. They just
thought that it must be normal on this planet
to leap out in front of someone and start
babbling away at a hundred miles an hour.
But although they were able to translate
what she said back into their own language,
they didn't understand a word of it.

"Hi, guys!" Kylie called. "Look, I know I've
already got your autographs about a billion
times already, but could you sign anyway?
I heard your single on the radio again by the
way! Just switched on and there it was! Well,
I mean, of course I switched it on, or else I
wouldn't have heard it! Ha ha ha ha! I heard
Blokezone's single as well and that's just
complete pants if you ask me! Yours is like a
trillion times better! And not only that, but

your haircuts are a billion times better and anyway do you think you could sign for me please?" She thrust her autograph book under their noses.

The aliens looked at each other. They wondered whether Kylie might be dangerous or not. She didn't look dangerous. Quite the opposite in fact. Kylie looked harmless and even rather friendly. She didn't look at all as if she was about to put the mission at risk. The aliens gave Kylie the all clear.

****

The aliens soon discovered that life on Earth was quite different from life on The Planet With No Name. But then it would be, wouldn't it? Let's face it, you don't hop into a spaceship, journey across space for billions of miles and expect to find somewhere exactly the same, do you? It's just not going to happen.

Having said that though, some things did seem strangely familiar. For a start, there was a McDonald's everywhere they turned. There were traffic wardens roaming the streets. And in the supermarkets, people were trying to sneak through the 'Nine Items or Less' checkout with ten items or more.

Soon, the aliens all came to the same conclusion. Earth was OK. It wasn't perfect, but they could see themselves living there.

Then again, anywhere was better than the last place they'd tried. That moon they'd found circling round the Earth – what a dump that had turned out to be. There was no water. There was no food. There was nothing to do. There was nothing to see. There was no atmosphere.

They could see themselves living on Earth though. OK, it was a little weird here and there. That crazy girl for instance. But then not everyone was like Kylie.

Anyway, they'd hang around a while longer and suss it out a bit better. They'd study and observe some more and prepare their reports for back home. It was really up to their bosses to decide if they'd all move here or not. It was up to their bosses to decide whether the search for a new home was truly over.

And if it turned out that the search wasn't over after all? Well, they'd just have to move on and try again. It wouldn't be the end of the world would it? At least they hoped it wouldn't be.

Chapter 5
Fridge

Live And Wicked! was a typical Saturday morning kids' TV show made up of endless cartoons, videos, competitions, interviews with soap stars, and above all else, loads of boy bands. A bunch of bored-looking ten-year-olds yawned and picked their noses in the background and there was a cheeky puppet called Brian The Beaver. The two presenters ran around grinning stupidly and forgetting their lines. But it didn't matter because *Live And Wicked!* was meant to be wacky and zany. Wacky, wacky, wacky! Zany, zany, zany!

The show's opening titles were wacky and zany! The studio set was wacky and zany! The camera angles were wacky and zany! Everything about *Live And Wicked!* was wacky and zany! Even Dave Pilchard, the show's 43-year-old producer, was wacky and zany! You could tell by the way he wore big pink-framed glasses and a back-to-front baseball cap. Wacky, wacky, wacky! Zany, zany, zany!

In other words, *Live And Wicked!* was just the same as a thousand other Saturday morning kids' TV shows before it. Well, almost the same. There *was* one difference. No other Saturday morning kids' TV show had ever had a cloned alien boy band appear on it before.

Live And Wicked! wouldn't have had a cloned alien boy band appear on it either if it hadn't been for Kylie. It was Kylie who'd spent days on end phoning all the radio stations, asking them to play *Groovy Groovy Yeah Yeah!* over and over and over again. If it hadn't been for Kylie, Stud-U-Like would never have made it into the Top 40.

Manager Ron Heslop had been drying the dishes and staring out of his kitchen window that Sunday evening when the phone rang. It was The Man From The Record Company, ringing to say that *Groovy Groovy Yeah Yeah!* had just entered the charts at Number 39.

"Right oh," said Ron in a calm voice like he'd just been told tomorrow was Monday. Ron put the phone down and started to dry the dishes again. It was a good ten minutes before the news sank in but when it did, Ron suddenly dropped his tea towel and ran out into the street, shouting at the top of his voice, "Number 39! Number 39!"

A little, old lady out walking her dog took pity on Ron and began to lead him gently by the arm. "You want Number 39 dear? It's down the other end of the street. I'll show you if you like."

But Ron was a man in a hurry. He couldn't wait to tell Mikey the news. He shook himself free and started to run. The little, old lady watched as Ron disappeared round the corner.

But when Ron reached the flat, he found that Mikey had already heard the news and was already in a state of shock. Well, Ron thought that Mikey was in a state of shock anyway. Why else would Mikey, along with Tony, Scotty, Lee and The Other One, be sitting, cross-legged on the kitchen floor, humming along with the fridge?

How could Ron know that he was really watching five aliens *thinking* to each other?

"I see you've heard the news then, lads?" said Ron. "Brilliant, eh?"

But the lads said nothing at all. They just carried on humming. Ron wondered if this was some weird, new craze that he hadn't heard about. After all, he'd got up to some pretty weird things himself when he'd been in Medicine Lighthouse back in the early 70s.

Ron decided to sit down and hum along with the fridge as well. The last thing he wanted was to appear fuddy-duddy and out of touch with young people. After all, he was now the manager of a Top 40 band!

****

Ron was flicking through the pages of a travel brochure when Dave, the producer of *Live And Wicked!* phoned him the next day.

"Hi! Is that Ron Heslop?"

"Might be," said Ron, wondering whether it was Tony, up to one of his tricks.

"Ron Heslop, manager of chart-busting new boy band, Stud-U-Like?"

"Very funny, Tony," said Ron. "Now get off the line will you? Somebody important might be trying to get through."

"Sorry?" said Dave, sounding puzzled.

"Look I know it's you, Tony," said Ron. "So be a good boy and get off the line before I come round there and shove that phone right up your ..."

"Mr Heslop, my name's Dave Pilchard. I produce a programme called *Live And Wicked!* Perhaps you've heard of it?"

"Pardon?" said Ron.

"I was wondering whether Stud-U-Like would like to come on next Saturday's show?"

"Er, yeah. All right then," Ron spluttered.

"Don't you want to make sure they're free first? You might already have a booking."

"Oh, yeah. I'll just check," said Ron.
He rustled the pages of the travel brochure, hoping that Dave might think that he was flicking through his diary.

"Next Saturday?" ... (rustle, rustle) ... "Next Saturday ... let me see now ..." (rustle, rustle) ... "yeah, that should be OK."

"Great!" said Dave. "My people will talk to your people about the details."

"OK," said Ron, wondering what on earth Dave was talking about and who on earth all these people were.

"I like you, Ron," said Dave. "Let's do lunch sometime."

Kylie nearly choked on her cornflakes when she switched on *Live And Wicked!* the

following weekend and saw Stud-U-Like
staring right back at her from her TV screen.
Well, the alien Stud-U-Like staring right back
at her anyway. But they looked so good!
Their eyes twinkled! Their hair was perfect!
They were just so drop dead gorgeous!
And they were dancing and smiling and
singing and everything!

But wait a minute. What was this? Stud-U-
Like *weren't* singing at all. They weren't even
opening their mouths. They weren't even
trying to mime along to the words! What was
going on? Surely they could hear the music?
Everybody else could! Why weren't the band
at least pretending to sing along? Kylie could
hardly believe what she was watching.
Neither could anybody else. Even the
bored-looking ten-year-olds in the studio
stopped picking their noses and started to
look a bit less bored. It was a disaster. It was
a complete nightmare. The beginning *and* end

of Stud-U-Like's career in three dreadful minutes.

They've blown it, thought Kylie. Their one big chance and they've blown it!

Then, just when Kylie thought she'd die of shame, the song ended.

There was a deathly silence in the *Live and Wicked!* studio. Nobody knew quite what to do. Then suddenly the two presenters started to clap madly. "Whoa! Yeah! Let's hear it for Stud-U-Like! Stud-U-Like, everybody!"

The presenters were grinning so hard, it looked as if their faces would split in two. Like they'd got wire coat hangers stuck in their mouths or something.

"Whoa! Are those guys wacky and zany or what?" said one of them.

Kylie held her breath. What was that? What did they just say?

"Whoa! Yeah! What crazy, mad, bonkers guys!" said the other presenter.

"Whoa! Yeah! Stud-U-Like! Wacky and zany! Wacky, wacky, wacky! Zany, zany, zany!"

Kylie let her breath out again and slumped back in her seat. So the band hadn't made idiots of themselves in front of millions of TV viewers after all! They'd known exactly what they were doing! They weren't being useless and rubbish. It was all just part of the plan. They were just being wacky and zany! Wacky, wacky, wacky! Zany, zany, zany! Of course! It was so clear now!

Kylie felt a huge wave of relief sweep over her.

I bet that was Tony's idea! thought Kylie to herself.

Tony was, after all, The Funny One.

Chapter 6
Tools

Of course it hadn't been Tony's idea at all. At least, not the real Tony's idea anyhow. The real Tony knew nothing about being on *Live And Wicked!* How could he? The real Tony was billions of miles away on The Planet With No Name.

Meanwhile back on Earth, the alien Stud-U-Like were hot news all of a sudden. *Live And Wicked!* had been their big break. Now everybody knew about these crazy guys who didn't even bother to mime along to their songs! Stud-U-Like were famous! They were big stars!

They might have been even bigger stars if people had known that they weren't the *real* Stud-U-Like at all. Funnily enough though, no-one noticed any difference. They looked exactly like the real Stud-U-Like and that was all that mattered to their fans.

Their fans didn't think to ask which planet they were from. They wanted to know other stuff. What shampoo did The Blond One use? What did The Cute One have for breakfast? What was The Funny One's favourite TV show? The question of whether the band was human or not just never cropped up. It was something the fans took for granted.

It was just as well for the aliens that their true identity did remain a secret. The last thing they wanted was for anyone to find out who they really were. Their mission would have been over in an instant.

They would have had to set off on their intergalactic travels again.

On the other hand, The Man From The Record Company would have been more than happy to discover who they really were. An alien boy band?! How amazing! Think of all the newspaper headlines! Think of all the magazine covers! Think of all the money.

As it was, the offers soon came flooding in. There were album deals, concert tours and TV shows. There were interviews and photo-shoots. There were Stud-U-Like posters, calendars and duvet covers. There were Stud-U-Like kitchen utensils, a brand of Stud-U-Like carpet stain remover and even a range of Stud-U-Like gardening tools.

In other words, it was everything Mikey had ever dreamed of. The *real* Mikey that is, not the alien Mikey. It was just a pity that the *real* Mikey wasn't around to see his dream come true. It was just a pity that the *real* Mikey was in a totally different part of the universe at the time.

But hey, that's showbiz.

Ron Heslop meanwhile, was a very happy bunny. And who could blame him? He was all set to make an absolute fortune. Ninety five per cent of all the band's earnings were going straight into Ron's back pocket!

"Why not?" thought Ron. "I put them together in the first place, didn't I? Without me they'd be nothing!"

Of course the boys needed to earn a living too, so Ron had kindly agreed to let them split the other five per cent between them. Well, he didn't want to appear greedy, did he?

Chapter 7

Girls

While most of the country went Stud-U-Like crazy, the band, or rather the *alien* band, just carried on quietly with their mission to find a new place to live. They had no idea of the madness they were causing. They had no idea they'd become so famous. They didn't even know what being famous meant!

Hardly a day went by now without the band being splashed all over one of the newspapers. The headlines were always either made up, or stupid. Sometimes they were both:

"MY ZIT HELL BY BLOND ONE!"

"FUNNY ONE IN NEW HAIRSTYLE SHOCK!"

"HARD ONE ATE MY HAMSTER!"

"CUTE ONE STROKES DOG!"

"MY STEAMY NIGHT OF PASSION WITH THE OTHER ONE!"

But being in the newspapers meant nothing to the aliens. They thought it was normal. They thought that was just the way things were on this strange, little planet.

They thought it was normal to be chased down the street by reporters and photographers, flashing away with their cameras.

They thought it was normal to have people fussing round, fetching chairs and

opening doors for you. Back on The Planet
With No Name, you normally did stuff like
that for yourself. Back on The Planet With No
Name, you normally fed yourself and dressed
yourself and bent down to pick up something
that you'd dropped. Here on Earth, it seemed,
there was someone to do all that for you.
Here on Earth, it seemed, you were never,
ever alone.

Then, of course, there were the large
packs of Earthlings who spent all their time
following the band around wherever they
went. Sometimes they even got there first.
And for some strange reason, they always
seemed to be the same *type* of Earthling.
The type known as Girls.

Stranger still, the girls always seemed to
be sobbing and screaming. Why did they
follow the band around if it made them so
unhappy? Why not just stay at home instead?
It was a mystery to the aliens. They didn't
understand it at all.

Mind you, there were plenty of other things that they didn't understand about Earth either. Like cricket for instance. What was that all about? Why hit the ball and then chase after it? It seemed crazy. If they didn't hit the ball in the first place, there would be no *need* to chase after it, would there?

But the whole point of the aliens' mission was to learn about Earth. They had come to discover whether Earth was a suitable planet to live on. So, for the moment anyway, the aliens tried not to worry too much about the mysteries of girls and cricket. There would be plenty of time for that in the future.

By now, the band had five different songs in the Top 40. *Groovy Groovy Yeah Yeah!* had become one of the fastest-selling singles ever. There was even talk of Ron's old group, Medicine Lighthouse, getting back together for a series of concerts. This was proving to be rather difficult to arrange though.

The singer was now a vicar, the drummer had been dead for 20 years, and Alan, the keyboard player, was now called Wendy and lived in Wales. This only left Ron Heslop and he was far too busy ripping off Stud-U-Like.

Stud-U-Like had now become so big that other boy bands were beginning to copy *them*. You could spot the copycat bands a mile off. There was always a Blond One, a Funny One, a Hard One, a Cute One and an Other One. And just like Stud-U-Like, they didn't even try to mime along to their songs either.

Kylie hated the way that everybody loved Stud-U-Like now. And she hated the way that everybody pretended they'd loved them for ages. Because Kylie really *had* loved them for ages. Long before they'd become famous. Much longer than anybody else. She'd loved them since they'd begun. Kylie had loved Stud-U-Like for a whole six months. And now everybody else loved them too. And she hated that.

After all, it was Kylie who'd waited all alone outside Mikey's flat for days on end. It was Kylie who'd hung around outside the studio day after day, hoping for an autograph. It was Kylie who'd made all those calls to the radio station asking them to play *Groovy Groovy Yeah Yeah!* over and over again. And did she get any thanks? No, she did not. But then it's never easy being an obsessive fan.

Kylie also hated all the bands who tried to copy Stud-U-Like. She thought they were all rubbish. Nothing like the real thing at all. They had neither the talent nor the good looks. Kylie thought they should all just give up. There was no point. There was only one Stud-U-Like.

Or so Kylie thought anyway.

Chapter 8
Sheep

Meanwhile, in a galaxy far, far away, the *real* Stud-U-Like had suddenly become hot news too. The Planet With No Name had never heard a band like them before. Up until then, heavy rock and thrash metal was all that they'd ever listened to. All the bands had long hair and wore lots of leather. Fresh-faced boys with floppy fringes and centre partings were an alien idea to them.

But now, thanks to Stud-U-Like, The Planet With No Name had simply gone boy band bonkers. They were all the rage. They were new. They were different. You could hear the words and there was a proper beat. If you were into boy bands you were seen as being hip and trendy. Heavy rock was last week's thing.

Crowds of screaming fans greeted the band wherever they went, chanting their names and holding up banners. They were showered with love and attention. They were treated like gods. They were given thousands and thousands of teddy bears and small, furry animals.

Mikey, Tony, Scotty and Lee were superstars on The Planet With No Name. But weirdly, the *biggest* superstar of them all was The Other One. The Other One was seen as the true leader of the band. The Other One was thought to be the only one with any talent. There was even talk that The Other

One was going to leave the rest of the group and go solo.

It was a funny, old world.

Mikey still didn't know how they'd come to be on The Planet With No Name. Or why it had happened. One thing was sure though. He might as well enjoy fame while it lasted. Why not? He might suddenly find himself zapped back to Earth again. Or even zapped somewhere completely different! No, he was here now. He was going to go for it.

So Mikey went for it and so did the rest of Stud-U-Like. The next thing they knew they were asked to perform on The Planet With No Name's longest-running TV show, *Top Of The Rocks*!

The band's performance on the show had the whole planet talking the next day. The way these boys moved their mouths to make it look as if they were singing along to the words! No-one had ever done that before.

What were they playing at? Were they mad?
Were they doing it on purpose?   But whatever
they were doing, it worked. It worked big
time! The Planet With No Name was buzzing.
And everyone agreed. Stud-U-Like rocked!

Of course, Mikey would have liked it a lot
better if Stud-U-Like had rocked their own
planet. But he had to admit, being famous
anywhere was pretty cool. It was, after all,
what he'd always wanted.

He didn't know it at the time, but Mikey
wouldn't be famous for long. Neither would
the rest of the band. They would soon all just
be faces in the crowd again. That's because
hero worship on The Planet With No Name
was a serious matter. Here, on The Planet
With No Name, the fans didn't just stick a
poster up on the wall, or wear a T-shirt.
Here, the fans would soon start to change and
morph themselves into their favourite Stud-
U-Like band member. Before long, there'd be
millions of Blond Ones, millions of Funny

Ones, millions of Hard Ones and millions of Cute Ones. And as if that wasn't weird enough, before too long, there'd be billions of Other Ones! Mikey and the guys would no longer be different. They'd look just like everyone else.

In a funny kind of way, that was exactly what was happening back on Earth too. Everyone was suddenly banging on about how all boy bands looked and sounded the same. Everyone was saying how you could swap one for another and never notice the difference. Everyone was accusing boy bands of being nothing more than a bunch of sheep.

Nothing more than a bunch of clones.

Chapter 9

Daggers

"Hello, Mikey. Remember me?" challenged Kylie in a way which showed that she was not to be messed with.

Kylie stood in the doorway of Stud-U-Like's dressing room, hands on hips and looking daggers. She'd managed to sneak past the security guy at the studio gate. It hadn't been difficult. He'd been fast asleep.

"It's me. Kylie. Your obsessive fan? I used to hang round outside your flat. You used to wave to me."

Mikey, or rather, alien Mikey, looked at Kylie. He'd seen her somewhere before. He did remember her. She'd been one of the first people they'd met. They'd thought she was harmless at the time. But now it seemed they might have been wrong. Mikey could sense that Kylie was angry. But why?

"What's the matter?" said Kylie. "Too famous to talk to me now, are you?"

Mikey and the rest of the aliens watched. They didn't know what to do next. As a matter of fact, Kylie didn't know what to do next either. She hadn't really expected to get this far.

"Don't you see that if it hadn't been for me you wouldn't be here now?" said Kylie. "It was me who phoned all the radio stations and got them to play your song in the first place! Without me you wouldn't be rich and famous at all. You wouldn't be sitting here, about to go on TV. You'd be nothing!"

"What do you think you're doing?" said a gruff voice. "Who let you in here?"

The smell of cheap aftershave filled the room. Then Kylie spun round and found herself face to face with Ron Heslop.

"It's OK," said Kylie, trying not to be sick. "I'm a fan. I just wanted their autographs, that's all."

Ron looked at Kylie through his tinted glasses and thought for a second. The kid seemed OK. Why not let her get what she'd come for? If she was really lucky he'd give her his own autograph as well.

"All right. But be quick. They're on in a minute," said Ron.

"Thanks," said Kylie, holding out a pen and a piece of paper.

Mikey, or rather *alien* Mikey, took the pen and looked at it for a moment. It was almost as if he was wondering what to write.

"How about, 'To Kylie'. For old times' sake?" suggested Kylie. "Oh by the way, that's Kylie spelt K-Y-L-I-E in case you've forgotten."

But *alien* Mikey didn't write anything at all. Instead he popped the pen into his mouth and swallowed it. Kylie stared at him. She knew that something wasn't quite right. But what?

Mikey stared back at Kylie and grinned.

"Why did you do that, Mikey?" said Kylie. "Tony's the one who eats pens. Tony's The Funny One. Isn't that right, Tony?"

But Tony said nothing. Instead, he picked up a pair of electric clippers and began to shave off all his hair. He looked mean and moody as he stared in the mirror.

"What's going on, Tony?" said Kylie. "You're not The Hard One! Scotty's The Hard One, aren't you, Scotty?"

But Scotty said nothing. He was in a world of his own, arranging a bunch of teddy bears into a nice, neat line.

Kylie looked at him in amazement. But Scotty just smiled sweetly and made one of the teddy bears wave at her.

"What are you doing, Scotty? You're not supposed to be The Cute One! Lee's supposed to be The Cute One! Aren't you, Lee?"

Kylie turned to Lee. But he didn't say anything. He didn't do anything either, except stand to one side and look a bit useless.

"This is mad!" yelled Kylie. "You can't just suddenly become The Other One, Lee! You can't just all suddenly swap places whenever you feel like it!"

The aliens looked at each other. Kylie was clearly much smarter than she seemed. It was time for them to leave.

"The kid's right," said Ron Heslop. "What do you think you're playing at? I'm the boss round here! I tell you if you can swap or not! And I tell you it's just not on. Scotty, give that flipping teddy bear back to Lee at once. You're The Hard One and that's how it's going to stay. And Tony, stop shaving your head and start being flipping funny again!"

Ron looked at Tony. It was too late. Tony was completely bald.

"Well, just make sure you grow it back as fast as you can," snapped Ron. "And from now on, no more swapping! Right?"

But there was no need for Ron to worry. There wasn't going to be any more swapping. In fact, very soon there wasn't going to be any more band. The aliens were going back to The Planet With No Name. Their work on

Earth was done. Their mission was complete. It was time for them to change back into plain, old aliens again. They were just getting a bit mixed up in the process, that's all.

The aliens sat down cross-legged in a circle and started humming along with the fridge. They needed to think to each other. Their cover had been blown. It was time to be moving on.

Ron seemed to sense that something odd was going on between them. "Look, lads, sorry if I was a bit harsh just then," said Ron. "It's just that well, you know ..."

But it was too late. The alien Stud-U-Like had begun to fade in front of Ron's and Kylie's eyes.

"Lads? Lads!" screamed Ron. "Look, if it's about the money I can explain everything! I'm sure we can work something out!"

But by now, the band had almost vanished. So too, had Ron Heslop's dreams.

"Come back, lads! Look, I'm sorry! I'm really, *really* sorry!"

It was too much for Ron to take. He threw himself headlong into the middle of the circle and along with the five aliens disappeared into thin air. Kylie had watched in horror. It was too much for her to take as well. But Kylie chose not to join Ron and the guys. She just fainted instead.

Chapter 10
More Pizza

Kylie opened her eyes. Everything still looked a bit fuzzy. What had happened? She tried to sort out her thoughts, but they still made very little sense.

Slowly it all started to come back. Kylie could remember being in the band's dressing room. She could remember being angry. There'd been that horrible whiff of aftershave. And a lot of shouting. And then? Then the boys had started getting all mixed up. Then there'd been more shouting ... then they'd started to disappear! Ron had tried to stop them and then *he'd* disappeared too! What on earth was going on? It was just too weird.

"Are you all right? You must have fainted."

The voice was soft and soothing. The breath smelt faintly of pizza.

"Here. Have a sip of water. It'll make you feel better."

Kylie took a sip. Slowly, she began to focus on the face above her. She saw a floppy, blond fringe and a centre parting. There was an angry-looking zit on a perfectly square jaw.

"But I thought you'd ..."

"Thought we'd what?" said Mikey, gently.

"Well, er ..." Kylie hesitated. "Disappeared."

"Yes, well, if it makes you feel any better, we don't know what's going on any more than you do," said Mikey.

"Phew, to think it was all just a dream!" said Tony, running his hand through his blue-streaked, spiky, black hair.

"What? A dream?" said Kylie.

"Just joking," said Tony, grinning.

"Shut up, Tony," said Scotty, head-butting the dressing-room door playfully.

"Mr Bear and I pretended that we went on a long journey to a faraway place, didn't we, Mr Bear?" said Lee. He made Mr Bear nod his head and answer in a big, deep voice.

"Yes, we did Lee!"

"I think what my fellow band members are trying to say is that some pretty weird stuff has been happening. We're all a bit confused at the moment," said The Other One.

Everyone turned to look at him in amazement.

"What was that you just said?" asked Mikey.

But The Other One didn't say a thing.

He was right, though. Some pretty weird stuff *had* been happening.

One minute, Stud-U-Like had been on stage in front of thousands of screaming look-a-like fans on The Planet With No Name. And the next? Well, here they were. Back on Earth again in their own dressing room.

It was almost as if they'd never been away. Well, not quite. Before going, they'd been just another struggling boy band. *Groovy Groovy Yeah Yeah!* had just been played on the radio for the very first time. Now all of a sudden they were huge. It was kind of difficult to take in. In fact it was so weird that it was probably best not to think about it too much.

It was probably best that Stud-U-Like didn't find out about the aliens anyway. And it was *definitely* best that they didn't find out that the aliens had given Earth a big thumbs-up. That way they need never know that they were about to get visitors. Plenty of visitors. Blond Ones, Funny Ones, Hard Ones, Cute Ones and Other Ones. Lots of Other Ones.

That was all in the future though.

"Don't suppose you've seen Ron, our manager, have you?" asked Mikey.

"Er, well ..." began Kylie.

"Tinted glasses?" said Tony.

"Terrible haircut?" said Scotty.

"Terrible aftershave!" added Lee, helpfully.

"Oh, him!" said Kylie, not sure what to say. "Yeah. He was here a minute ago."

But at that moment, there was a knock on the door and a young woman with a clipboard rushed into the dressing room. "Hey, guys, you're on in five minutes," she said. "Follow me."

More Teen Titles!

Barrington Stoke would like to thank all its readers for commenting on the manuscript before publication and in particular:

James Allum
Jason Kevin Amor
Andrew Baillie
Kimberley Carroll
Lindsay Clarke
Charlene Coll
Charlotte Curran
Harriet Curran
Mary-Anne Curran
Rob Darling
Jack Davidson
Jimmy Dean O' Brien
Laura Donachy
Michael Fawcett
Ian Ferguson
Timothy Fielder
Stephanie Harper
Adam Harrison
Caroline Holden
Diane Hooper
George Lei Hutten

James Johns
John Labert
Caroline Loven
James McIlhargey
Roddy Macleod
Kirsty Maclean
Mark Malcolm
Chris Oldham
Andrew Pringle
Marcus Richards
Daryl Robin
Julia Rowlandson
Lisa Sellers
Matthew Stacey
Sam Standen
Peter Stevens
Luke Sully
Craig Taylor
Stewart Turner
Hayley Wilkinson
Mark Williams

Become a Consultant!

Would you like to give us feedback on our titles before they are published? Contact us at the address or website below – we'd love to hear from you!

Barrington Stoke, 10 Belford Terrace, Edinburgh EH4 3DQ
Tel: 0131 315 4933 Fax: 0131 315 4934
E-mail: info@barringtonstoke.co.uk
Website: www.barringtonstoke.co.uk